THE LOVELY ONE

Lee Aucoin, *Creative Director*
Jamey Acosta, *Senior Editor*
Heidi Fiedler, *Editor*
Produced and designed by
Denise Ryan & Associates
Illustration © Vicky Fieldhouse
Rachelle Cracchiolo, *Publisher*

Teacher Created Materials
5301 Oceanus Drive
Huntington Beach, CA 92649-1030
http://www.tcmpub.com
Paperback: ISBN: 978-1-4333-5649-0
Library Binding: ISBN: 978-1-4807-1748-0
© 2014 Teacher Created Materials

WRITTEN BY
SHARON CALLEN

ILLUSTRATED BY
VICKY FIELDHOUSE

Contents

Chapter One

BELOVED

When Beloved's mother first saw her
lovely baby giraffe, she looked at its four
strong legs. She said, "Those legs will take
you on wonderful adventures." She looked
at her baby's lovely big eyes and said, "Those
eyes will see amazing things."

She watched her baby sleep on the first night after she was born. She murmured, "My baby is so sweet and dear. I will name her Beloved because she is. And she will be beloved forever."

Beloved was a tangle of legs when she first tried to walk. On her first day, she learned to stand without falling. When she stood next to her mother, Beloved was already as tall as her mother's hips. Beloved's mother taught her to stand tall, to know that she was beautiful, and to be kind.

Beloved and her mother spent all their days and nights together. Sometimes, they went walking. Sometimes, they went exploring with the other giraffes. Sometimes, they just watched what was happening around them in the beautiful highlands of Africa.

All the other animals admired the giraffes. No other creatures had such long necks, long legs, or long tongues!

Chapter Two

AN AMAZING PLAN

The General of Egypt wanted to give the King of France a very special gift that would help unite their countries. The general asked his advisor what the king would like more than anything else in the world.

"There is nothing more beautiful than a giraffe," his advisor said. "The King of France has never seen a giraffe. Let's send him one!"

"Hah! We live in Africa. France is on the other side of the world!" said the general. "How can a giraffe go from Africa to France?" he asked.

"I think I have a plan," replied his advisor. "The first step is to choose the loveliest giraffe in Africa."

"What about Beloved? She is said to be the loveliest giraffe ever," said the advisor's assistant.

"Fetch her!" said the general. And so the advisor and his assistant traveled to the deepest parts of Africa to find Beloved.

When the men found her, Beloved was heartbroken to be taken from her mother. Her huge eyes were full of tears.

"Don't you want to see the world?" the advisor asked Beloved. "Don't you want to meet the King of France? You will have a wonderful adventure."

Beloved still was not sure. However, her mother said, "I told you, those eyes will see amazing things. You must go."

It was time for the next part of the advisor's plan. Beloved would go to the Nile River. Then, she would sail up the river to the coast of Egypt to meet the general.

Beloved's mother watched sadly as the advisor lifted young Beloved onto the back of a camel. But she knew her baby had a wonderful adventure ahead of her. Then, the camel plodded for five days to the river. There, Beloved was gently loaded onto a sailing boat.

Giraffes do not often sail. At first, Beloved was not sure she liked it. But soon, the things she saw along the riverbanks began to interest her. She saw farmers tilling the rich black soil and people fishing with spears and nets.

After many days, the boat reached the coast. The general came to meet the boat. The advisor was certain the general would like Beloved. Indeed, when the general first saw Beloved, he smiled in delight. She was truly lovely. She was the perfect present for the King of France.

Beloved lived at the general's palace for three months. Each day, she grew taller and stronger. Finally, she was strong enough to make the long trip.

It was time for the next part of the advisor's plan. Sadly, he said goodbye to Beloved. His job was with the general. Two animal handlers would care for her now.

Chapter Three

SAILING TO FRANCE

Even though Beloved had traveled so far, she was still in Africa. Now, she had to cross the sea to France. She traveled in the hold of a ship. Three cows traveled with her to give her all the milk she needed. Three sheep and an antelope also kept her company.

The animal handlers did everything they could to make Beloved happy. They cut a hole in the roof of the animals' pen so Beloved could put her head through it and see outside. They put straw around the hole to make it soft for her neck. They made a sunshade to keep Beloved cool and dry.

After sailing for three weeks, they arrived at a port in the south of France. It was still a long way from the king in Paris. How would they get Beloved from the port to the king? Beloved would have to walk! But, the animal handlers knew Beloved was not yet ready to walk so far.

France was too cold, and Beloved was still very young. She needed to grow even stronger. She would have to practice each day until she could walk to Paris. Every day, Beloved and her handlers walked through the countryside. She drank lots of milk and ate apples, bananas, and dates. With each walk, Beloved grew stronger and fitter. Finally, at the end of spring, she was ready for her long journey.